paper hands

paper hands

PATRICK HOBBS

dancing blue

p a p e r   h a n d s
First published 2001 by Dancing Blue Press
Falcons, Barkers Hill, Semley, Shaftesbury, SP7 9BH

ISBN: 0 9540195 0 4

This book is a gathering of poems from the years 1985 - 2000.
Some of these poems first appeared in the following publications:
University of Bristol Newsletter, *Rhubarb Rhubarb*, *Artyfact*, *Other Poetry* and *Departures* (Housman Society 1998).

Printing by Bookcraft (Bath) Ltd, Midsomer Norton
Cover design by Lydia Knights
Front cover image by Lydia Knights and Patrick Hobbs
Back cover photography by Chris Howse and Patrick Hobbs

Thanks to Chris, Coral, Gay, Jenny, Joseph and Lydia

For Martin and Karen

contents

"I am interested in one thing only, and that is grace..."

LES MURRAY

A Letter to Elizabeth Jennings

Reading your poems I sense you
Lifting stones and finding
Beauty like water
Beneath. And I think I see you
Walking your brown road
Where you have picked up thousands -
From axe-edge flints to pebbles
Rounded like eggs,
Known their weight and hardness,
Bruised and bloodied your fingers.
You know what it is to be pierced,
To be bled of all but the blackness;
And quietly
You walk away from bitterness
To tread like a shy diviner,
Always sensing this stream that runs
Alive, unseen, redemptive;
The moments of grace that hide
Under each day's hurting.

Violet Street

A corrugated landscape, clay
Folded into streets, our valleys
Little red-brick canyons
Crowded between slate ridges,
Dark roofs sloping to sky,
Sometimes holding, like pewter,
A dull reflection of blue.
The sun rolls round its high
Grey shelf and eyes
Reach up like hungry children,
The violets still in hiding.

Derby, October 1992

Newcastle Train

She haunts the corner of my eye -
Her white ankle live and shining
Above the dark suede boots,
Her young legs in slate-black jeans.
Beside me a Scot, red hair and glasses,
Notes train numbers at York,
Then returns to his Bible
And the first chapters of Galatians.
To my right slow flashes of yellow -
The Van Gogh fields of foreign rape,
Brave stands of huddled cowslips,
Gorse alight with flower.
And in my head crystal thoughts;
Of Italy, fireflies, the hills,
And of my bright young niece
Alive in my arms this morning.
In my lap now a novel
Of three and a half deaths
And love
Ever after.

Joseph at Bethlehem

He remembered how nine months
Earlier he came in
And heard before he saw
The whisper of her skin on the clay,
The rustle and whirr of her skirts,
The slap of cloth on a kitchen wall;
Birdsong slipping slow and silver
Down the slope of evening;
Her face angled to the window,
Terracotta shattered on the floor,
And between the fragments of supper
In the half-light Mary, dancing.

Domani

Jerusalem, like some dry ship,
Pushes her way out into mid-July,
An ocean of heat closing behind her.
Still sea-sick I stumble
Through voyagers and hawkers,
Armed orphans, barefoot seekers,
Past videos lining a cave -
Their hooded titles waiting in darkness.
The Hospital of the Myrrh-Bearers
Open as an offering,
Reggae skanking in the door
Of a gift shop, and eyes
Where nothing gives.
Then some Italians, pilgrims toiling
Up a sloping deck, men turned
By years, but the tongue still dancing -
'Domani, ecco! Domani, domani...'

Jerusalem, July 1992

Brunacci's Harvest

A sudden dream of rain,
Hard to believe
Below this roof of heat;
Rain vertical and shy, a thin
Leak and the roof holds.
Brunacci is down in his field,
Hauling in bales that lie like cars
Tumbled from the road above.
Last week he brought in his corn -
Beneath a hooked moon the combine
Dwarfed the waiting trailer,
And hunched like a cow to suckle her calf,
Poured out the grain, silver, smoking.
He turns stiff shoulders against the slope
As a fiercer shower begins,
His wife calling from her umbrella,
Her shouts bending the rain.

Santa Maria Lignano, Italy, July 1994

Signora Brunacci

Signora Brunacci brings eggs,
Warm round facts of life
Given in an oblong basket.
Her husband six weeks dead,
And the hens still lay, the sheep
Still lead her under the olives.
The kindness she meets
Is only his echo
Between the stones and the hills
Where she leans waiting for his voice,
His hands -
His clay hands now folding like leaves
Back to the earth they fought.

Casa Rosa, Italy, May 1997

Thinking of Bosnia

A hundred vague flies and
Spiders' silk curving in the light;
A birch hangs sudden yellow now
Amid the green, and the air,
The air is like water, needing
The sun to warm it. And while trees
Fill fruit before turning in
Our new world map is bleeding,
A haemorrhage of human beings
Too close to our autumn wealth.
So we draw inside, close the windows,
Wash our hands, and nurse
Our own slow angers.

Plaxtol, Kent, September 1992

Refugee

Called by a name I cannot own,
Pinned in a long car, my world
A railway, my head numbered;
I am held by angled rails.
Mother railway, why
Are there guards on your doors?
And always this examination
Of the pockets of my heart -
What can I say
Of my home or destination?

Trinity
after three paintings by Tom Hammick

Facing a painted ocean
We look for islands, smudges of reference,
Landfalls of memory, hills
To anchor the shifting skyline.
Space so intense it scrapes us;
Three skies open and we grope
For the reassurance of walls,
Or stand in a place like prayer,
The mind on a cliff-edge leaning
Out and over the sea.
Only the wind in our face
Keeps us from falling, as the arms
Of horizons embrace us,
Measuring us up for heaven.

Irina Ratushinskaya

You stand,
Bear-square but quietly rooted,
A coal-scuttle helmet of a hairstyle,
Clothes that look cut for housework.
In this hall tonight you seem to have come
From somewhere out-side of fashion;
And I search for unfashionable words -
Like humility, like grace;
And find myself unwinding
Tired definitions of both.
Gathered, in something like shyness
You read, but second,
Letting your translator lead.
Gently you joke about your sons,
Born together after prison doctors
Swore they had killed your womb -

This fierce and intimate power to create,
A gentleness that will not lie down.

The Essential Moment
for Henri Cartier-Bresson

You recognise the unnoticed,
Within the black edge of a negative
You cradle the essential moment,
The crucial millimetre's gesture
Held in geometries of light,
Architecture of sun and stairways,
Simply seen and loved.
A worker asleep on his shipyard bench,
Four boats strung down the Rhine,
A Frenchman striding on to water -
The diary of an eye available
To the human signatures of days,
Your shutter seizing the gift of the immediate,
Kissing the fraction of a second.

For Les Murray

Round as a bar prop,
Your geometry totally opposed
To the gaunt garret type
We imagine a poet.
Yet circles describe your view -
From the rich and thirsty earth
And the physical syllables
You roll in your mouth like tobacco,
To a mother's death, a child's moon,
The things that are wordless -
Without ever needing to close
The circle,
Let alone to square it.
Yours is a voice that does not close;
Listening to dreams and silence,
You call the words to the pages
Like your cattle brought in for milking;
A rolling creation story
That you go on telling.

Rain

The rain is slow now,

Slow as the heron's arched wings.

Evening falls with leaves.

And You

And you, you, you, why you -
Your warm new sap in my shy veins,
My empty hands in the leaves of your hair,
Your touch that lays moonlight
Across my land...?

You Live Beside Water

You live beside water, a place
Where you sit, never allowing
Me further than your shore.
I stand, I swim, I tremble
At the electric grace of your body,
And find myself retreating
Back across this river;
Only to come again and again -
Wet and sliding, treading
The razor stepping-stones,
Clumsy in square, black shoes.

One morning in dream-time
I will come
Barefoot, like a dancer.

Poem from Hospital

They wrap the bricks around my window,
And still the day flies in.
Last night I pulled down a star,
Held it,
Out of October's sky.
Between drug-mists I remember the hills,
My thoughts spin out imagined freedoms,
And still the day flies in.

The Same Shoes

Six years on, your hair seems darker -
I don't remember you so beautiful.
I wear the same shoes, leaking now,
And there are other holes - your kiss
Surprises them like water.
I remember how you read The Windhover,
Singing his kestrel, giving me
Wings into poetry and evening -
Do you remember the evening, the bird?
Your card I keep for the ochre glow
Of its photograph and your words
On the back - 'Good luck,
Especially
In the important things...'

Swallows

When your voice faded
I sat and watched the swallows,
Saw you among them.
I picked up our fallen words,
Tried to lay them to rest.

This stand-off tonight -
You in a cage, hiding yourself;
I, struggling to open,
Confused as a man
Who tries to make a bird fly.

Losing My Arms

I am losing my arms, they are paper
Breaking in a heavy sea;
They are paper filled with hot stones.
I am losing my arms as one loses
Love - the pain
An empty weight that burns and burns.

Plaxtol, August 1994

Holes

September now, and quietly
The sun is falling apart.
In the day's low corners I meet
Her holes in me, the scars
Ripening like apples.

Three Fish

In my hands three fish,
Shining pewter, curving full,
Wet with a petrol sheen - smears
Of violet, blue and gold;
Trout that have bathed in rainbows.
Unfolding from a late sleep
I wake to them here in my hands,
I wash them gently, stroking
A tilted fin, and the long hole
Where the knife found and emptied the guts.
In my hands three fish,
The still-wet weight of grace
And the given-ness of things.
I bow my head in gratitude,
My whole mind kneeling
As I take the knife again.

After

I cannot stretch the years out -
Time for me is not linear,
Life does not live in straight lines.
The months curve like moons,
Like links in a loose chain
Folded back on themselves.
There are afternoons when I walk
Next to me six years younger,
And there are nights
When still I lie
So near to you, make dreams with you
In the curve of the moon,
The bend of the years -
These years that curl now like a whip.

White

In my thoughts she will always be
In white, on a hill with a bird
And two dark butterflies
Singing at her shoulder;
Rain and honey, a small tree swaying
Golden in the morning.
She shivers, and the wind loves her,
Lifting her hair as she turns again
And leans away from me,
Making friends with the sand and the snow
That blow in under her feet.

Silver

Outside I can hear

The owl's blue cry, trembling, silver -

A door in the night.

For a Friend

Yes, there were days when this
Might have tried to be
A love poem;
But no, not now, not now.
They seem short and round -
These years of shifting in
And out of each other's lives,
Not always close, not always clear.
And you, sometimes warm as honey;
Sometimes in a distance learned
From your father, or your uniform.
But I've known you come undone
After a night-shift,
Or down a telephone line -
A sudden unravelling like wool,
And you have held me in tears now;
A touch like old rain,
Bathing the years, the expectations.

Milan

I rode into Milan on the back
Of Anna's Yamaha, clutching
Her nylon anorak, so shy
Of her delicate waist; so shy
Of all of her I wandered
In a sharp and sleepless cloud
With joy at every edge -
Past crucifixions at the gallery,
And Leonardo's divine supper
That feeds the bombed church,
Jazz by canals, a guitar,
And the books on her bedroom shelf,
To the compartment of the Switzerland train
And the blindness of goodbye.

Two

after a painting by Alan Feltus

How many afternoons
Have we sat together,
Or turned to lie and listen
To the music in this room?
My head now covered as if in prayer,
My hands gathered in this book,
I am with you and apart -
Our intimacy a pattern
Of parallels half-naked,
A searching modesty,
A shy confession.

For Toby on His Ordination

The loom was alive here -
Shuttles singing,
Colours choiring together,
Bright strands flying loose
For the next years' harder weaving.
Your father stayed on his knees as we turned
To sit - the circling prayer
Gathered on a hundred unclean lips
Seeking the Spirit's kiss,
A burning coal, the washing
Of his shining rain.

Derby, September 1992

Psychiatric

Hospital towel wrapped round his head,
Mornings he used to lie,
The dark shroud of his anorak
Hauled to his chin or further.
He spoke of needing to chain-saw
All the trees and burn them.
He was quiet, like broken glass
Floating in a tight green sea.
Days he paced the corridor,
Stopping as he kissed
The locked doors at each end.

To Sam on His First Birthday

I wanted to send you leaves -
Enough to bury you in yellow
And a thousand shifting shades
Of ochre, brown and red.
Autumn cannot be posted,
And these words will mean nothing to you,
But words are built of crooked letters,
Shapes full of holes,
Where love,
Like leaves,
Slips down to earth
And little people on the floor.

Amber Valley, Derbyshire, October 1992

On Cley Beach

Skimming stones,
I stoop at the tide's edge
As each small wave breaks to leave
A moment's flat water behind.
And behind me, above me, you stand -
Tall, quiet, singular,
Holding yourself, collected;
Your coat of pain wrapped close about you,
Printed with his violence, wet
From the wound you want to hide.
Nervous of touching you,
I bend by the water
Or scamper back, wet-toed,
When a wave plays rougher;
Bending and shifting between
You and the sea, the sea.

For David

I know the nights of wire and glass,
The cracks in the morning through which
Our lives shout back at us,
The acid days when beauty
Withdraws like the frightened plover.
And I know that you are too alive
Not to feel, like the bird,
The shadows that test our freedom,
A searching fear as the silhouette
Of a sparrowhawk edges the field.
Then as threats recede
To leave their questions
Green space embraces again
The wheeling ballet of wings,
The mysteries of grace returning.

For Sasha

I know you only
From tears in another's eyes,
The ebb of her voice
As your death came and settled,
A bird on an upturned heart.

Eight years young and blind
From a sickness of old men,
Strange cells take you away
And all our words turn foreign,
The truth so thick we stammer.

There is wisdom here
You alone can clearly see,
A small completeness;
A circle joined, your sisters
Round you, your last soft word of thanks.

Daniel's Gift
after a painting by Lani Irwin

His hands surprise me with their patience,
Brushing the crest
Above my eyes, the slope
Of my bowed head.
I see him rich as a bee,
His baskets full of pollen,
Dancing a honeyed secret.
I feel my hair, tied back
Tight and long, a rope
For Daniel as he stretched
To visit the roof of me.
And I do not want to move again -
The balance of my child's touch
So delicate in my hair,
The butterfly in my hand,
I lean between gifts
So weightless
They hold me.

Ice

I walk on thin ice,

The water black and boiling,

My feet in dancing shoes.

Valnerina

The forests, painted churches,
Our skin like a veil
Suddenly thinned by the light,
And we recognise every bone,
The map of the day's caress.
Beauty touches holes
In us, and as each shy window
Opens we begin to see.
How often the details of truth
Remain invisible,
Yet the land teaches us,
And we become like mirrors
Angled to each other
Reflecting a wider light -
The walls of our days shining ochre,
Blue,
Soaked with the colours of frescoes.

Nera Valley, Italy, June 1998

Love Song

I do not want to undress you;
No, I want to clothe you,
To pull the breeze of your shirt
Over your saving landscape,
The watered hills of your breast,
The warm slow fields of your back
That are white now as for harvest;
To sing your skirt's dark waves
Round the cool shore of your waist,
Spin you in a circle tide
And listen to your legs
As they whisper to each other;
To gather your hair, your hair,
And the small and necessary mysteries
You hold within like a tree;
To cover your lines, your colours,
This image of God as seen
Through water, a gift
So full that only silence
And heaven can hope contain it.

Three things I will never tie on you,
Three I will always remove -
Your two shoes and the little clock
That bruises your wrist like a coin.

His Feet

I knew the laws, the throne,
The anger to which they tied him.
They took him and nailed him in a book
That ate my nights and my heart.
Yet in the aching evenings
I have heard the stones cry out,
And I have met him dancing,
The grass singing between his toes.
And in his dance seas are involved,
Mountains can move, and trees
Will clap their thin, chapped hands.
Nothing that I have met in this life
Is as green or as bruised as his feet.
Nothing is so young.

The River Broken

We divided the river early,
Up by the spring, hard on the source,
Cutting bold new channels down
And pulling the stream apart.
Brave work it seemed, like felling forests,
Building cathedrals, a kingdom.
We trapped the force in our separate canals,
Chained the wild flow in a hundred ditches -
This water that is old as heaven
And young as the blood of God;
A love that would strip a man
And leave him naked, alive,
Strangled now in our pipes,
Broken in shallow pools.
I have watched waves and rivers,
Have stood by seas and seen
How water longs for water,
How deep calls to deep,
Frozen puddle to mountain falls,
How the river yearns, leaning to the sea,
How the cloud gives itself to the source.
In this evening now I kneel,
Looking for rain, longing to gather
Our wounded streams together in welcome,
Bring all our rivers home.

The Blue Field

An arm's length of blue between us,
We walk in a tractor's tram-lines,
These machine-cut arcs you feel
As scars and which I read
As part of the composition.
From the ridge it seemed a lake,
And we circled the field of flax
As people circle water,
Drawn to reflected light,
Then stepping in to bathe.
And I feel I should go barefoot -
To wade unshod through flowers,
An orphan touching home.
But we brave the dust of pesticides,
Grieve for butterflies, and speak
Of God, of mountains,
And the violence and joy of friendship.
You say things which unlock me
And I tread behind you now,
Dropping fragments of my past,
My future into the patient
Blue of the field, the moment's
Simple wealth awaiting
The heart's archaeology.

Dust

There are times when I wait and he comes,
Quietly over the fields
And into my evening watch,
Slipping between the words
I have held out to him.
Like water he unclothes me;
Stooping to uncurl
My clawed fingers, he writes
In the dust that I hold in my hands.

God

And there are holy spaces
Meetings I cannot contain
Or touch
Even as my hand cannot grasp
The wrist on which it pivots

The Moors
for Martin

I stood above Sheffield, praying
The moors to come, embrace us;
Forests to rend their clothes and lay
Every new leaf at your feet,
Wanting to wring God's rainbow,
See all the colours
Bleeding down the sky.

6th September 1997

for Martin, died 26th May 1995

And I needed this for you,
Your beauties no less deserving
This crazed royal farewell -
A nation halted in flowers,
The motorway a car park,
Aisles of tarmac and blossom;
A country bared and weeping.
Aircraft pulled out of the sky,
Postmen stopped in tears,
The scattered salutes of policemen;
Bells muffled, the clocks
All still, the day
Holding your death in both hands.

Death of a Brother

I saw you shoulder your doubts against
All the bright edges of November,
Your feet still trailing poems down pavements;
Then afternoon's darkness melting in the theatre
As flamenco span and coursed through your veins.
I knew your winter when you turned from fighting,
Tried to wash your dreams in the rain,
Then collapsed in a chair, the sores of your anger
Anointed by Arvo's cleansing psalm.
I was hiding in the South, frightened,
A tender traitor to love
The nights when demons fingered your mind
And drummed on the skin of each taut minute;
The mornings when you woke as if caged, on camera,
Every motion judged and failing.
You could not live in the house of our answers,
Nor sleep in the bed your God had made you.
Rising, you pushed through the arms of angels,
And before I woke to shop for your birthday
You emptied the ampoules into your pain,
Took quiet death in your arms,
Lay down beside the morning.

Prayer

To kneel again at the broken window,
My arms, my paper hands
Aching out to heaven,
Slowly collecting silence,
Glimpsing
In the shards the reflection
Of the God who comes up behind me.

Muddy

'The glory of God is a human being fully alive'

And so to be children, growing
Younger into our humanity.
Born between thorn and nail,
We must live now, here -
Eyes wide amid the hurting;
Daring to find a love
Deep in the poison garden,
Learning our steps in the barefoot way,
Dancing muddy into eternity.

notes

A LETTER TO ELIZABETH JENNINGS *(page 11)*
Elizabeth Jennings is one of the finest, truest English poets of the last 50 years.

TRINITY *(page 20)*
The three paintings were abstract seascapes which together made up a triptych, a single work.

IRINA RATUSHINSKAYA *(page 21)*
The Ukrainian poet Irina Ratushinskaya was arrested in September 1982 for writing poetry. She was imprisoned and then sentenced to seven years hard labour in a prison camp. She continued to write poems, some of which were smuggled out of the Soviet Union at great risk. In October 1986 she was released and allowed to come to Britain. KGB doctors had told her that due to the torture and deprivation she had suffered she would never be able to have children. In February 1992, in London, she gave birth to twin boys. The poem was written after a reading she gave in London some 8 months later.

THE ESSENTIAL MOMENT *(page 22)*
The Frenchman Henri Cartier-Bresson was arguably the greatest photographer of the 20th century (though he fiercely disputes this praise). In his book 'The Decisive Moment' he wrote 'photography is a simultaneous recognition, in a fraction of a second, of the significance of an event, as well as of a precise organisation of forms which give the event its proper expression'.

FOR LES MURRAY *(page 23)*
Les Murray is Australia's leading contemporary poet.

THE SAME SHOES *(page 29)*
The Windhover - by Gerard Manley Hopkins (1844-1889), perhaps the most electric poem in the English language.

MILAN *(page 39)*
Leonardo's divine supper - the astonishing fresco of the Last Supper by Leonardo da Vinci on the wall of the chapel of Santa Maria delle Grazie. In 1943 Allied bombing almost destroyed the church and the painting was badly damaged.

HIS FEET *(page 52)*
Line 10 echoes a poem by my godmother, the poet Sheila Barclay.

THE RIVER BROKEN *(page 53)*
The poem takes as its starting point the gift of God's Spirit in John 4:14.

6TH SEPTEMBER 1997 *(page 58)*
This day saw the funeral of Diana, Princess of Wales.

DEATH OF A BROTHER *(page 59)*
Arvo's cleansing psalm - the music of Arvo Pärt, the contemporary Estonian composer, which touched my brother profoundly.

MUDDY *(page 61)*
'*The glory of God is a human being fully alive, and a human life is the vision of God.*'
- St Irenaeus, Bishop of Lyon (130-202 AD).